The Holmes Sutra

A birthday gift for Sherlock Holmes
as he turns 160

Jayantika Ganguly

Paperback ISBN 9781780925356
ePub ISBN 9781780925363
PDF ISBN 9781780925370

Published in the UK by MX Publishing
335 Princess Park Manor, Royal Drive,
London, N11 3GX

www.mxpublishing.com
Cover design by www.staunch.com

To

Sherlock Holmes

Idol. Inerrant. Inspiration.

Contents

Foreword

Of course, there is no justification at all why I should be writing this foreword; I'm clearly quite unfitted to be doing so as I scored only 17 on the Holmes Mania Quotient test (you'll find it towards the end of the book). By contrast Jay Ganguly is clearly not only suffering from StockHolmes Syndrome (the most extreme form of the mania) but well out the other side and on her way to... well, whatever place addicts go to when Holmes has taken over their lives.

My score tells me that I am merely Sherlocked, which is fine by me as I fell in love with Irene Adler as portrayed in the Sherlock TV series. (If you've no idea what I'm talking about, then you definitely need this book).

So, despite Jay's poor decision to select me as the writer of the Foreword to this sutra (oh dear, reader, are you like me and find that the only Sutra you can recall is that of the Kama variety? But Wikipedia tells me that sutra means a collection of aphorisms, which is exactly what this it. So no titillation here!) I am delighted to do so.

Well of course Sherlock Holmes and the many people he encountered are part of the fabric of London and its environs, which is where I live. When did I first encounter him? No idea – you might as well ask me when I first heard the violin. But there is no doubt he is part of our national psyche – and even more delightful is that he has been embraced in so many other countries.

At one level you can read this book purely for amusement. If Watson's accounts amount to a few volumes, his work has spawned whole libraries of books, as well as extensive coverage on TV and film. Holmes pervades the media and the many references that Jay has found may even encourage you to widen your exploration of the genre - and thereby raise your Holmes Mania Quotient.

This is also a work of scholarship, with a considerable bibliography that will direct you to many sources that certainly were new to me (but remember, I am merely Sherlocked).

But best of all, enjoy the sutras. They are a mixture of observations drawn from the accounts of his adventures, and propositions either put by Holmes himself or drawn from a reading of Watson's accounts. They illuminate the characters of Sherlock Holmes and John Watson; they reflect the times in which they lived; and above all, they speak to us of the human condition.

Calvert Markham

London

September 2013

Introduction

Sherlock Holmes, the greatest (and the most popular) detective the world has ever known, turns one hundred and sixty on 6 January 2014 – or so we believe, thanks to the great Christopher Morley, who not only founded The Baker Street Irregulars, but also gave our favourite 'Consulting Detective' his birthday (Doyle 284). In fact, a celebration in New York City is organised every January – dates for the next round are 15 January 2014 to 19 January 2014 (BSI 2014 News). The Annual Dinner of the Sherlock Holmes Society of London also occurs around this period – dates for this time are 11 January 2014 and 12 January 2014 (SHSL).Now, a decade over one and a half centuries is no laughing matter – Sherlock may be divine and immortal for those of us in the know (which, presumably, refers to a significant portion of the living human population on earth at any given point of time) – but a hundred and sixty years is impressive, you have to admit.

So, to commemorate this milestone, and to join in the celebrations of his birthday, from the erstwhile 'colonies' of the Indian sub-continent (oh yes, we love him, too), I present to you – "The Holmes Sutra", being no more and no less than one hundred and sixty aphorisms (well, sort of – they are more like a neon green thread of comic relief running through the Sherlockian fandom) inspired by Mr. Sherlock Holmes (and his various avatars), with a brief explanation (hopefully) of each, and a test of your 'Holmes Mania Quotient'.

The Holmes Sutra consists of two parts:

1. *The Mantras*

   This part consists of one hundred and sixty mantras (sayings, slogans, mottos, aphorisms, *Sherlockisms* – call them what you will) which have been based on, related to and/or inspired by Sherlock Holmes – not just the original books, but various literary and media adaptations as well.

2. *The Holmes Mania Quotient Test*

   Are you Sherlocked or Holmesick? Or something else? The second part includes various sub-categories of 'Holmes Mania' – finally classified and defined, together with a basic questionnaire to gauge *your* Holmes Mania, based on your HMQ score. Also discusses the possibilities of a cure. (This section is not recommended and is strictly meant for optional reading. It is being included merely to appease a certain set of people that shall remain unnamed).

As far as this author is concerned, Sherlock Holmes is real and immortal – of course, my parameters of reality are slightly different, and several non-canonical materials appear true as well. However, all adaptations have not been accepted as true – some are clearly works of fiction (besides, we have to consider that (a) if we take *everything* as true, we would be left with gaping inconsistencies, and (b) the number of Sherlockian adaptations are too many for a person of my meagre skills to track down and review). Primary references are, obviously, to the canon (Christ abbreviations), followed by <u>Sherlock</u> (BBC).

Happy birthday, Sherlock Holmes. Hope you like this gift.

The Holmes Sutra: Part I

The Mantras

1. ***Sherlock Holmes is as 'real' as you or I.***

And if that is something you cannot agree with, this would be a good time to stop reading. (I can only apologise for the good money you spent on this book – but well, maybe you could pass it on to someone?) What defines reality? What defines existence? Is mortality the sole determining factor of reality? Should logical faculty, influence, adoration and devotion not be factors? If we go by the *cogito ergo sum* argument (Descartes 4-5), he thinks, therefore he is real. Besides, if brilliant Sherlockians like Leslie Klinger treat the canon as biographies (Klinger, Vol.3 xiii-xiv), who are we to argue?

2. ***The cure for Holmesickness is to find your Holmes.***

Holmesickness: A psychological condition where the patient complains of mental trauma and quite often, also suffers from associated psychosomatic aches, when completely deprived of the company of Sherlock Holmes in any form for an extended period of time. It may be noted that the illness may manifest regardless of whether the abstinence is voluntary or forced.

To ascertain whether you suffer from Holmesickness or some other form of Holmes Mania, please refer to Part II and get your Holmes Mania Quotient (HMQ) score.

3. *'The Science of Deduction' (STUD, Sherlock: ASIP) is a refined art.*

Yes, yes, I can hear the protests, and yes, I know Holmes said, "Detection is, or ought to be, an exact science, and should be treated in the same cold and unemotional manner. You have attempted to tinge it with romanticism, which produces much the same effect as if you worked a love-story or an elopement into the fifth proposition of Euclid," to Dr. Watson (SIGN); but do remember that he also remarked (GREE), "Art in the blood is liable to take the strangest forms." Dr. Watson (VALL) did say, "He was always warmed by genuine admiration – the characteristic of the real artist."

To be honest, great artists and great scientists are not all that different. Genius is genius, no matter what form it comes in. And who can deny Sherlock Holmes' genius?

4. *When you have eliminated the impossible, whatever remains, however improbable, must be the truth.*

The Master said it (over and over, in various avatars) – not I (SIGN, Sherlock: THB, Elementary: Leviathan). Even Commander Spock believes in it (Star Trek)!

5. *If you cannot locate the data you require, it is cleaning time at your Mind Palace/Brain Attic.*

I am certain Sherlock cleaned his Mind Palace (Sherlock: THB)/ Brain-Attic (STUD, FIVE) regularly. The attic's structure is how our mind works (Konnikova 26) – it needs to be maintained.

6. *Dr. John H. Watson is every bit as remarkable as his companion.*

Not only did he accompany Sherlock for his adventures and chronicled them, he weaned the detective off his cocaine addiction (MISS). The good doctor is also adept at gleaning information out of his friend – of course, Sherlock sees through it, amused, but nonetheless divulges the information sought by John (Meyer, Canary 30).

7. If Sherlock is your home (Holmes?), John is your hearth – and wall.

"Directors simply don't know what to do with Watson," complains Estleman (Estleman vii) – and until a few years ago, this was unfortunately true. John is a doctor and a soldier, a killer and a healer – a paradoxical bundle of talents unto himself, and most certainly not the endearing but bumbling simpleton he is sometimes portrayed as (SH-Washington, SH-Death). Thankfully, Jude Law (Sherlock Holmes, Sherlock Holmes: Game), Martin Freeman (Sherlock) and Lucy Liu (Elementary) have rectified the image. There can be no incandescent Sherlock Holmes without John Watson – he is the conductor of light, remember? "It may be that you are not yourself luminous, but you are a conductor of light," Holmes tells his companion (HOUN). John stimulates Sherlock's genius.

8. Everyone, especially a genius like Sherlock, requires a partner to bring them their entitled glory.

"I hear of Sherlock everywhere since you became his chronicler," Mycroft Holmes says to Dr. Watson the very first time they meet (GREE). Be it the chronicles published in *The Strand Magazine* or a blog, Watson brings Holmes his glory.

9. ***Mediocrity knows nothing higher than itself, but talent instantly recognises genius.***

Dr. Watson speaks of Inspector McDonald (VALL), but it is as applicable to the good doctor as anyone. Consider this (IMDB, <u>Sherlock: ASIP</u>):

> "Dr John Watson: [after Sherlock has just explain his working out of Watson's veteran status, his war wound and his sibling's drinking problem] That... was amazing.
>
> Sherlock Holmes: You think so?
>
> Dr John Watson: Of course it was. It was extraordinary. It was quite extraordinary.
>
> Sherlock Holmes: <u>That's not what people normally say.</u>
>
> Dr John Watson: What do people normally say?
>
> Sherlock Holmes: "Piss off"..." (emphasis added)

10. *John Watson is an excellent role model.*

    Strong moral fibre, nerves of steel, bravery of a soldier (Sherlock: ASIP), unflinching loyalty (Sherlock: TRF), overqualified medic, protective streak (Sherlock: TBB) – what is there not to admire and emulate?

11. *Sherlock Holmes is more than just a man – he is a just man.*

    Hope, the cabbie in Sherlock: ASIP, was wrong, of course, when he says, "You're just a man..." Besides, an unjust man could not have permitted Dr. Sterndale (DEVI) or Captain Crocker (ABBE) to walk free.

12. *Your own Holmes is where your metaphorical heart actually is – in your mind.*

    Where else would the Master reside except his favourite place? The rest of your system is just an appendix for him, anyway. In his own words, "I am a brain, Watson. The rest of me is a mere appendix." (MAZA)

13. *The veneer of 'a calculating machine' (SIGN) is a defence mechanism.*

Sherlock, for all his poise, is not only vulnerable, but cares for his friends as well – we see proof of this in the way he reacts at John's heartfelt praise when he rattles off his deductions for the first time (Sherlock: ASIP) and whenever John is in danger (Sherlock: TGG and TRF, 3GAR).

14. *The lowest and vilest alleys in London do not present a more dreadful record of sin than does the smiling and beautiful countryside (COPP).*

The sentiment is a little appalling, yes, but you cannot dispute the logic Holmes puts forth – peer pressure, fear of sanction and ease of discovery are each valid points.

15. *Sherlock remains stubbornly human despite our attempts to deify him – a phenomenal human, a hero, but human, nonetheless.*

"Don't make people into heroes, John. Heroes don't exist, and if they did, I wouldn't be one of them," he says (Sherlock: TGG). And though his conduct may be worthy of a Vulcan (Star Trek) at times (Sherlock: THB), he remains human – the "best and wisest man" (FINA) and "the most human human being"

(Sherlock: TRF). Sherlock Holmes is one of the most human literary characters (Kasius 13).

16. **Learn from the Master, S.O.D. everything, i.e. See, Observe and Deduce.**

"Eyes and brains," says the animated, defrosted Sherlock (Sherlock Holmes in the 22nd Century) to his companions, the policewoman Beth Lestrade and the robotic Watson.

17. **Sherlock Holmes would be lost without John Watson.**

"Good old Watson! You are the one fixed point in a changing age," Holmes says to Dr. Watson (LAST). Sherlock quips – a little sarcastically, but with a grain of truth, "I'd be lost without my blogger." (Sherlock: TGG) – a play on the slightly more sincere "I would be lost without my Boswell." (SCAN)

18. **Curiosity, unsatisfied, eventually dies a death of boredom (Meyer, West 6).**

This gem is actually from Dr. Watson. So, if curiosity kills the cat and unsatisfied curiosity dies of boredom – the cat dies either of curiosity or of boredom. It appears as paradoxical as Schrödinger's Cat

(Wikipedia, Schrödinger's Cat). All right, that made more sense in my head than on paper.

In any case, we are a patient lot – we are "The Fandom That Waited", after all (Sherlockians: TFTW).

19. ***Sherlock Holmes is the only one in the world (of his kind).***

This is a bit obvious and does not really require an explanation, does it? He says so himself (SIGN, Sherlock: ASIP) – though he speaks in the context of his chosen profession. I like to generalise it a little more. Don't you think so?

20. ***If your mind is like a racing engine, apply the brakes slowly and gently. Do not, under any circumstances, resort to drugs – it will only make you race faster and off-course.***

Sherlock Holmes' career was endangered, remember (MISS)? Poster boy for anti-drugs campaigns, our Mr. Holmes.

21. *Holmesian truths are often stranger than fiction and more fantastic than fantasies.*

As Holmes says, "Life is infinitely stranger than anything which the mind of man could invent." (IDEN) Sometimes, the adventures are so incredible that our heroes assume mythical proportions and when Watson promises to put down the truth in his writings, Holmes laughs, saying no one would believe it. (Meyer, <u>West</u> 4)

22. *The frailty of genius – it needs an audience. (Sherlock: ASIP)*

"Appreciation, applause, at long last – the spotlight!" Sherlock tells John (<u>Sherlock: ASIP</u>), explaining the murderer's psychology and how the clever ones are desperate to be caught. All the misunderstood and/or unacknowledged geniuses out there will agree.

23. *Do not guess – await adequate data; you cannot make bricks without clay.*

We know what Sherlock thinks of guessing (SIGN) - "It is a shocking habit – destructive to the logical faculty." Before you begin to hypothesise, you need information – as they say, a little knowledge is dangerous. To quote Holmes, "It is a capital mistake to theorise before one has data. Insensibly one begins to twist facts to suit theories, instead of theories to suit facts." (SIGN) and "Data! Data! Data! I cannot make bricks without clay." (COPP)

24. **Sherlock Holmes has a heart – and a sizeable one, at that.**

Moriarty knows (<u>Sherlock: TGG</u>). Mycroft knows (<u>Sherlock: ASIB</u>) when he says, "My brother has the brain of a scientist or a philosopher, and yet he elects to be a detective. What might we deduce about his heart?" Dr. Watson knows when he gets shot (3GAR) and Holmes panics. Dr. Watson observes, "For the one and only time I caught a glimpse of a great heart as well as of a great brain."

25. **Sherlock Holmes is immortal.**

No, he is not a vampire – no offence to Count Dracula (Stoker 13), but 'undead' and 'immortal' are different.

26. *There is no remedy for StockHolmes Syndrome –*
the good news is that you would not suffer from it
(though your significant other might).

StockHolmes Syndrome: A psychological condition
where the patient exhibits maniacal collecting
tendencies towards any media, object or discussion
referring to, or in connection with Sherlock Holmes.
Early symptoms include being Sherlocked (<u>Sherlock:</u>
<u>ASIB</u>), obsessive acquisition of Holmesian goods
such as Sherlockabilia (Sherlockology) and incessant
quoting of dialogues from various Holmesian media
during conversations. Further details (and your
diagnosis) can be found in Part II of this book.

27. *Great men of Holmesian character stand alone.*

Mycroft calls him a "lonely, naive man" (<u>Sherlock:</u>
<u>ASIB</u>), Dr. Watson talks of (MAZA) the "gap of
loneliness and isolation which surrounded the
saturnine figure of the great detective." and Dr.
Watson's second wife refers to his loneliness (Fields
152, 546).

28. *Consider every wretched hive of depravity and murder in this city, my place of business.* <u>*(Elementary: Pilot)*</u>

Why would you limit yourself to one city, Sherlock? The world is your playground. This danger extends to the associates of Sherlock Holmes as well – and this is why Dr Watson learnt to keep his matrimonial life a secret, after his first wife is murdered and the second nearly so (Kuhns, <u>Untold: The Solved Problem</u>, 187, 199). Holmes and Watson may love the thrill of danger, but they want to keep their loved ones safe.

29. *Believe in Sherlock Holmes.*

John does (<u>Sherlock: TRF</u>, Watson, Blog). I am sure you must have heard of the #BelieveinSherlock Movement – it is phenomenal (Asher-Perrin, Believe). There is a Tumblr page devoted to the movement, too. And while you are checking that out, it may be a good idea to look up #Moriartywasreal as well.

30. *Innovation, invention, technology, resources – you need each of these to complete your task properly.*

Sherlock makes good use of the latest technology whenever he can – take the record player and dummy to fool his enemy (MAZA), the pencil lead shavings to trace a fingerprint (Norbu 34-35), the smart-phone and the expert consultant Raz (Sherlock: TBB). It is beneficial to use all tools at hand.

31. *Sherlock Holmes can perform magic. Literally.*

The enigma, the ascetic nature – hidden depths have always been hinted at. So, when he is at the Ice Temple of Shambala, protecting the young Lama and his new Bengali friend, forming *mudras* with his fingers as though he has been doing it all his life (Norbu 250), we are not really surprised.

32. *The canon is real, and true – though not always accurate.*

Yes, there are inconsistencies and mistakes – but Dr. Watson is human, too. At one point, Watson dismisses some of the canon - LION, MAZA, CREE, 3GAB - as forgeries and drivel (Meyer, Seven 17), which I do not really subscribe to (he was quite old when he wrote it, after all, maybe it slipped by).

33. ***Sherlock Holmes is not an imposter in any form whatsoever.***

There has been a host of literature and media on this issue, which though interesting, are clearly flights of fantasy. Some claim that the real Sherlock Holmes died at Reichenbach (FINA) and an imposter came back in EMPT (Klinger, Vol. 2 818-819). In one instance, Watson has been depicted as the real mastermind, with Holmes being an impoverished actor hired to play the great detective (Without a Clue).

34. ***You can be the perfect reasoning machine – but that does not mean you are not a passionate person.***

Consider these words of Dr. Watson:

"The ten years since his death have provided me with ample time for reflection upon the question of Holmes' personality, and I have come to realise what I always really knew - but did not know that I knew - that Holmes was a deeply passionate human being. His susceptibility to emotion was an element in his nature which he tried almost physically to suppress. Holmes certainly regarded his emotions as a distraction, a liability, in fact. He was convinced the play of feelings would interfere with the precision demanded by his work and this was on no account to be tolerated." (Meyer, Seven 14)

Holmes expressed similar feelings when Watson announced his marriage (SIGN).

35. *If Sherlock Holmes and Mycroft Holmes went bad, the world would be doomed.*

And here we thought Big Brother and Thought Police (Orwell 2) were the nadir of dystopia. Though, after Khan (Star Trek: ID), I have to admit Sherlock would be the classiest villain ever. "It is fortunate for this community that I am not a criminal," Holmes says (BRUC), and truer words were never uttered.

Then we have Mycroft, the man who is the 'British Government', according to his brother – the power in those hands can only be imagined by us. Mycroft is the one man who can observe more than Sherlock –

what would we do if that magnificent brain turned to crime, instead? We can only hope his "decidedly somnolent" nature continues (Dexter 1) – or that he continues to appreciate the "Problem of Induction" (Terjesen 238).

36. *The genius (and insanity) of Moriarty – the Napoleon of Crime, the Consulting Criminal – is as true as Sherlock Holmes.*

I do not subscribe to the criminal genius of Moriarty being a myth of a delirium-riddled mind (Meyer, Seven 23, 60). However, a meeting of Dr. Freud and Holmes may have a grain of truth. The complete truth, however, remains elusive.

37. *You get by with a little help from your friends; no matter how great you are, you need them.*

The Beatles got it right. Dr. Watson, the best friend you could ever imagine, disposed of the foul cocaine addiction that threatened to destroy Holmes' mind as well as career (MISS). Dr. Freud may have had a hand in helping Holmes out of his addiction, too, who knows? The mutual admiration of the two remarkable men rings true (Meyer, <u>Seven</u> 131) though we may never know the truth.

38. *Consistency and resolution are important...till a superior solution presents itself.*

"Getting Holmes to change his mind once he had got hold of an idea was like trying to reverse the direction of the global orbit," the good doctor complains. "...An idea would fix itself in his brain, take root there, and flourish like a tree. It could not be uprooted, only felled - and this only when struck by a better idea." (Meyer, <u>West</u> 3)

39. *Sherlock is a soul with many reincarnations.*

Adaptations, reincarnations, avatars – call them whatever you prefer. Whether it is a Holmes frozen in time and awakened in a later century (<u>The Return of Sherlock Holmes, Sherlock Holmes in the 22nd Century</u>), or transported in time by black magic (<u>No Place Like Holmes</u>), or a modern Sherlock born in the twenty first century (<u>Sherlock</u>, <u>Elementary</u>), the soul remains one – and no matter what form he takes, we shall always worship him.

40.   *Do not underestimate the importance of a non-occurrence.*

As the Master says, "Only one important thing has happened in the last three days, and that is that nothing has happened." (SECO) Of course, we all remember the curious incident of the dog in the night-time (SILV).

41.   *Individuals vary, but percentages remain constant.*

"While the individual man is an insoluble puzzle, in the aggregate he becomes a mathematical certainty. You can, for example, never foretell what any one man will do, but you can say with precision what an average number will be up to. Individuals vary, but percentages remain constant," Sherlock Holmes states (SIGN). Self-explanatory, really – I have nothing to add.

42.   *Sherlock Holmes wrote the book of life.*

It is the literal truth. Well, after a fashion – remember the article Watson dismisses as "ineffable twaddle" (STUD)? It was called "The Book of Life" and was anonymously authored by Sherlock Holmes. Why, what did you think I meant?

43. *Mycroft Holmes is the most powerful man you will ever know.*

Like his brother, Mycroft Holmes is unique – more than a man; he is an idea, a concept, a personification of the British Government (BRUC, GREE). His speciality is omniscience (BRUC). He is the most dangerous man you will ever meet (Sherlock: ASIP). And there is only one person who can challenge Mycroft – in his own words, "It would take Sherlock Holmes to fool me." (Sherlock: ASIB)

44. *Sherlock and Mycroft care for each other.*

It is apparent. Holmes turns to Mycroft for assistance when dealing with the evil Professor, and later, during his hiatus. He tries to impress his older brother with his deductions (GREE). From the mild sibling resentment depicted in some works (The Private Life of Sherlock Holmes) to the full-fledged sibling rivalry in others (Sherlock), the dynamics of the Holmes brothers has always been a cause of speculations. The affection, however, cannot be disregarded.

45. The sexuality of Sherlock Holmes has been, and will always remain a mystery.

Watson's second wife may tell us tales of their homosexual love (Fields, <u>My Dear Watson</u>), Holmes may fall for a beautiful female enemy (<u>The Private Life of Sherlock Holmes</u>), he may have an ambiguous love-hate relationship (or a whisper of one) with Irene Adler (<u>Sherlock: ASIB</u>, <u>Sherlock Holmes</u>, <u>Sherlock Holmes: Game</u>) or an *affair de Coeur* with The Woman (<u>Elementary: Woman, Heroine</u>), but we never really know for sure. As Moffat says, "Sex is brainwork for him. Can you imagine romance with Sherlock? He'd poison his girlfriend just to see if it works." (Hall 9)

46. If you love your work, you will not only enjoy it, but it will be a reward in itself.

Sherlock "lived for his art's sake" (BLAC) and believed "my profession is its own reward" (SPEC).

47. Boredom is dangerous.

A bored Sherlock results in bullet holes on Mrs. Hudson's walls (<u>Sherlock: TGG</u>, MUSG) or indulgence in a seven percent solution of cocaine

(SIGN) or insulting John and Mrs. Hudson (<u>Sherlock:</u> <u>THB</u>). Either way, a "bit not good".

48. **_Scotland Yard – or New Scotland Yard – adores_** **_Holmes (well, mostly)._**

They named their national computer system for major crime enquiries after him - Home Office Large Major Enquiry System or, HOLMES – how much more of a homage can you expect, really? We can leave aside the likes of Anderson and Donovan, of course (<u>Sherlock</u>).

49. **_Smoking is injurious to health._**

Very, very cliché, yes, but true, nonetheless – even Sherlock has substituted cigarettes with nicotine patches (<u>Sherlock: ASIP</u>), only smokes when in great distress (<u>Sherlock: ASIB</u>) and goes cold turkey (<u>Sherlock: THB</u>). That said, the pipes look supremely cool, don't they?

50. **_Sociability is overrated, and unusual persons are_** **_often unsocial._**

"I was never a very sociable fellow, Watson, always rather fond of moping in my rooms and working out my own little methods of thought, so that I never mixed much with the men of my year... my line of study was quite distinct from that of the other fellows, so that we had no points of contact at all," Sherlock confesses (GLOR). Mycroft, a similarly gifted genius, is one of the "most unsociable and unclubbable" men in London (GREE) – that is what the Diogenes Club is for at Pall Mall (Duncan 33).

51. ***Melodrama and subtlety are both important; you have to know when to use what.***

The Holmes brothers have a flair for the dramatic; it is obvious in most actions they take (<u>Sherlock: ASIP</u>) – but both can be very, very subtle when required, and play their cards very close to their chests (<u>Sherlock: TGG</u>). In <u>Sherlock Holmes: Game</u>, Holmes remarks, "It is so overt, it is covert." Not one of my favourite dialogues, no, but it is rather funny. Sherlock can be a bit of a drama queen at times, though – in his own words, "I never can resist a touch of the dramatic." (NAVA) Drama is the spice of life, after all (Ganguly, <u>Drama</u>).

52. *Sherlock Holmes has one sibling – Mycroft Holmes.*

The world would not be able to take any more, honestly. There is some recent speculation that the young Quartermaster (Skyfall) is a third Holmes brother (Q Holmes). According to Springer, there is a younger sister, Enola (Springer). According to Baring-Gould, there is the eldest, Sherrinford. While the existence of each of these siblings is well-reasoned and well-argued – I do not subscribe to these.

53. *Sherlock Holmes is definitely masculine.*

No offence to the literature devoted to a female version of the detective, but, as Bragg says, "A character rife with contradictions, Holmes is ideally suited to organize and reconcile differing models of masculine behaviour, yet also to interrogate and ultimately police normative masculine values." (Bragg 3)

54. *Mrs. Hudson is a long-suffering woman.*

Dr. Watson makes this statement in DYIN. Imagine a tenant like Sherlock. No matter how much you adore him, he would drive you "up the wall with his carryings-on" (Sherlock: TRF).

55. ***Sherlock and John – an epic bromance.***

A very fashionable word – "bromance". I am unsure of its origin, but the word has wormed its way into common parlance, and I feel it describes the two adventurous men's much-speculated and sometimes innuendo-ridden relationship perfectly. Moffat and Gatiss often are masters at playing on this – note the only dialogue of Sherlock: Season 3 that we have been shown so far – "The thrill of the chase...the blood pumping through your veins...just the two of us against the rest of the world." (Deen, BBC preview)

56. ***Sherlock can be very, very manipulative.***

Much to poor Watson's discontent – note how the detective plays his friend in DYIN and in Sherlock: THB. Let us not forget poor Agatha (CHAS). The underlying reason may be excellent, but it is rather cruel to manipulate your friends, especially John, in this manner.

57. *Sherlock Holmes is a good sport.*

It is evident from his good-natured defeat at the hands of Irene Adler (SCAN), or when his conjecture turns out wrong in YELL.

58. *Sherlock Holmes is a man of prodigious talent.*

He is a musician, he is a first-rate actor, he is good at fighting and he is a master of deduction. He may be "spectacularly ignorant" (Sherlock: TGG, Watson, John H. Blog) at some things – Dr. Watson's list in STUD gives us a good pointer – but in the end, he is still pretty amazing, is he not?

59. *Learn to work out the balance of probabilities.*

Take heed of the Master's words, "We balance probabilities and choose the most likely. It is the scientific use of the imagination." (HOUN)

60. *Despite the occasional prejudiced comments, Holmes is a fairly secular person.*

If he was not, would he have his "Baker Street Irregulars" (STUD, SIGN) or his "Homeless Network" (Sherlock: TGG)? Dr. Watson often refers to how people from all walks of society visited Baker Street (STUD, DYIN).

61. *Beware of exceptions.*

"I never make exceptions. An exception disproves the rule," Holmes says (SIGN). I suppose we could take this with a grain of salt – because most rules, theorems, laws that we know of have specified exceptions.

62. *Be ready to learn, always.*

As Holmes says, "Education never ends, Watson. It is a series of lessons with the greatest for the last." (REDC) Wise words from a very wise man.

63. *Everything has an explanation – if something does not, it just means we have not found the correct one yet.*

"There should be no combination of events for which the wit of man cannot conceive an explanation," Holmes observes (VALL). He lives by it, which would explain why he is so successful.

64. *What one man can invent, another can discover.*

And this is how Holmes deciphers the cryptogram in DANC and Sherlock: TBB.

65. *Sometimes, it is easy to miss the obvious.*

I can vaguely recall a rather old television advertisement making a statement to this effect. In any case, Sherlock observes, "There is nothing more deceptive than an obvious fact." (BOSC)

66. *Occam's razor works: often, a simple explanation is the best.*

"Perhaps, when a man has special knowledge and special powers like my own, it rather encourages him to seek a complex explanation when a simpler one is at hand," Holmes confesses (ABBE). Jim Moriarty exploits this weakness of Sherlock, too – "That's your weakness – you always want everything to be clever," he taunts (Sherlock: TRF).

67. *Silence is important.*

"You have a grand gift for silence, Watson. It makes you quite invaluable as a companion," Holmes compliments his doctor (TWIS). Of course, the good doctor punches him in a modern adaptation (Sherlock Holmes). One of the first things Sherlock confesses to his potential flatmate is that sometimes he is silent for days on end. (STUD, Sherlock: ASIP)

68. *Pay attention; small things are important.*

It is one the Holmesian maxims that Sherlock repeats several times – "It is, of course, a trifle, but there is nothing so important as trifles." (TWIS) A similar statement is made in BOSC.

69. *The links, the chain of events, the sutra – that is what you need to get to.*

To quote Sherlock, "As Cuvier could correctly describe a whole animal by the contemplation of a single bone, so the observer who has thoroughly understood one link in a series of incidents should be able to accurately state all the other ones, both before and after." (FIVE)

70. *Sherlock is cool.*

Tell me, who else can pull off, "My name is Sherlock Holmes. It is my business to know what other people don't know." (BLUE) or "The name's Sherlock Holmes and the address is 221B Baker Street." (Sherlock: ASIP)?

71. *What you do in this world is a matter of no consequence. The question is what you can make people believe you have done. (STUD)*

These words would be the most valuable pearls of wisdom for any professional in any field. I know of fairly successful people who know next to nothing about their chosen profession, let alone have any sort of expertise – who have risen through the ranks because the powers-that-be believed them to be "doers" and I have seen insanely knowledgeable and talented people fall into a career rut because they have failed to advertise their brilliance. This is your key to success. Holmes has hit the nail on the head – as usual.

72. *Violence has its own price.*

In a poetic mood, Holmes comments, "Violence does, in truth, recoil upon the violent, and the schemer falls into the pit which he digs for another." (SPEC)

73. *Some amount of laziness is required for innovation.*

Why would you bother inventing anything if not to save yourself some labour (Ganguly, Doormats)?

Sherlock can be very lazy, too. He confesses to Dr. Watson quite early on, "I am the most incurably lazy devil that ever stood in shoe leather - that is, when the fit is on me, for I can be spry enough at times." (STUD)

74. **Sherlock Holmes occasionally demonstrated the characteristics of a BUNDY (Ganguly, _BUNDY_) soul.**

BUNDY is an acronym for but-unfortunately-not-dead-yet and is used for people who often find themselves contemplating the motive of their existence, sometimes accompanied by bouts of depression and self-destructive behaviour. Consider Dr. Watson's words:

"Even the triumphant issue of his labours could not save him from reaction after so terrible an exertion, and at a time when Europe was ringing with his name and when his room was literally ankle-deep with congratulatory telegrams I found him a prey to the blackest depression. Even the knowledge that he had succeeded where the police of three countries had failed, and that he had outmanoeuvred at every point the most accomplished swindler in Europe, was insufficient to rouse him from his nervous prostration." (REIG)

Sherlock's prolonged drug-use, his bouts of depression, all seem to indicate his BUNDY tendencies. I wonder how much he would have scored on the BUNDY test (Ganguly, <u>BUNDY</u>).

75. *Discussions are essential.*

Sherlock observes, "Nothing clears up a case so much as stating it to another person." (SILV) Dr. Gregory House, a character inspired by Holmes, uses the process of differential diagnosis to treat his patients (<u>House M.D.</u>), which involves discussions with his team.

76. *Uncertainty is painful.*

In Holmes' own words, "Any truth is better than indefinite doubt." (YELL)

77. *Never reveal all your tricks.*

Remember how Dr. Watson goes from awe to "How absurdly simple!" in DANC when the chain of deductions is explained to him? As Holmes says,

"Results without causes are much more impressive."
(STOC)

78. *Focus – if you do not, you will end up running around in circles.*

"It is of the highest importance in the art of detection to be able to recognize, out of a number of facts, which are incidental and which vital. Otherwise your energy and attention must be dissipated instead of being concentrated," Holmes explains (REIG).

79. *Obstacles are invigorating; they force you to use your brains.*

Note Sherlock's glee when he says, "There is nothing more stimulating than a case where everything goes against you." (HOUN)

80. *When you make Plan A, you keep Plan B in reserve – when you think of Solution A, you should also have alternate Solution B, and possibly, Solution C.*

Alternatives are useful, and important. There can be multiple solutions to any given problem, and you will not arrive at the correct one unless you examine the alternatives as well. As Sherlock observes, "One should always look for a possible alternative, and provide against it. It is the first rule of criminal investigation." (BLAC)

81. *Unofficial knowledge is of paramount importance.*

"What I know is unofficial; what he knows is official," Sherlock says (ABBE). What would you choose? (Remember, knowledge is power.)

82. *Apply logic to your conjecture, and your hypotheses will progress accurately.*

Ground rule provided by Holmes, "When water is near and a weight is missing, it is not a very far-fetched supposition that something has been sunk in the water." (VALL) Consider your facts carefully, and then apply logic.

83. *It is a pity neither Sherlock nor Mycroft saw fit to pass on their genes.*

Not for lack of offers, I am sure – Sherlock did get propositioned by a ballerina (The Private Life of Sherlock Holmes), which he refused, landing poor Dr. Watson in trouble. There are tales of Mycroft's children, however, that are quite believable (Rector, Plaidbaby) and some of Sherlock's off-springs (Bangs, MaybeAmanda and OneMillionAndNine).

Whether there is any truth to these stories, I cannot say. However, in the absence of any evidence to the contrary, I choose to treat these as stories, for any child of a Holmes would be too remarkable to remain unknown to the world.

84. *Sherlock has even joined forces with the legendary Tom and Jerry – that is how versatile he is.*

Have you seen it (Tom and Jerry Meet Sherlock Holmes) yet?

85. *Sherlock Holmes: Consulting Detective, Harbinger of Justice to Criminals.*

"I am not the law, but I represent justice so far as my feeble powers go." (3GAB)

86. *The dilemma of great minds is that they are in need of constant stimulation.*

"My life is spent in one long effort to escape from the commonplaces of existence," Sherlock complains (REDH). He explains is drug addiction with, "My mind rebels at stagnation." (SIGN)

87. *Despite his cold exterior, Holmes cares for his clients.*

He is distraught when he thinks Sir Henry has been killed (it turns out to be Selden) in HOUN, he swears to avenge Hilton Cubitt in DANC and he shows a glimpse of filial affection for Violet Hunter in SOLI.

88. *Sherlock is capable of great sacrifice – though he would say he considers it logical.*

He jumps off a rooftop to save his friends (Sherlock: TRF). "…if I were assured of the former eventuality I would, in the interests of the public, cheerfully accept the latter," he says to Professor Moriarty, choosing his own destruction for the greater good (FINA). As Commander Spock says, "The needs of many outweigh the needs of one." (Star Trek: ID)

89. *Sherlock can be very sweet and charming when he chooses to be.*

Oh, he can act charming – he is an alarmingly good actor – but he can make genuine sweet gestures as well – note how he names his new bee (*Apis watsonia*) after his friend and colleague (Elementary: Heroine).

90. *Irene Adler is the ultimate femme fatale – she is The Woman.*

She has taken almost as many avatars as Holmes himself. To Holmes, she is always The Woman (SCAN). She is "the woman who beat him" – literally (Sherlock: ASIB). She is his one true love (Elementary: The Woman). She plays with him, he plays with her. Sometimes one wins, sometimes, the other. *C'est magnifique.* She is, allegedly, the mother of Hamish Watson Holmes, fathered by Sherlock Holmes, but I am a little sceptical about this particular off-spring of Sherlock.

91. *Sherlock makes extraordinary philosophical statements at times, almost as if he knew something monumental was about to happen.*

Remember when he says, "Now is the dramatic moment of fate, Watson, when you hear a step upon the stair which is walking into your life, and you know not whether for good or ill." (HOUN)

92. *There is but one step from the grotesque to the horrible. (WIST)*

Too true, as the adventure proved.

93. *Sherlock Holmes can perform extraordinary physical feats.*

Three days of absolute fast (DYIN), escaping from an inescapable prison (Thomas, Execution), climbing the sheer walls at Reichenbach (EMPT) – it boggles the mind.

94. *Sherlock Holmes may have had an eidetic memory, and quite possibly, synaesthesia.*

Dr. Watson notes, "The powers of memory exhibited by Sherlock Holmes would have been worth a whimsical monograph of the kind that only he could write. How any human being could have so encyclopaedic a recollection of so many diverse facts was beyond me, and I no longer sought the answer. Once he had tried to explain it by saying that the only thing necessary was a passion for knowledge which made it impossible to forget. Then he tried to define it as a system, in which knowledge of one thing led by association to two more – and so on by geometrical progression. It seemed far simpler to accept that once his indomitable memory learnt a fact, he never forgot it." (Thomas, Bly 166)

95. *It is never too late to learn new arts and crafts.*

Holmes learnt yoga and further arts of disguise from a sadhu in Banaras (Riccardi 6-7) during his hiatus after FINA.

96. *The Holmes brothers just would not leave poor John (or his notebook) alone.*

He keeps finding post-it notes from Sherlock (which are expected, more or less) and even Mycroft in his case-notes! (Adams)

97. *Sherlock likes to show off.*

"Without further ado, my companion supplied me with the most striking illustration of those powers for which he is justly famed, a fine example of the contingent value of the obscure," says Dr. Watson. (Symonds, Boer 124) Another example would be the bedazzling of poor Henry Knight in Sherlock: THB.

98. *Genuine appreciation is always welcomed.*

Holmes is touched when Inspector Lestrade says, "I've seen you handle a good many cases, Mr. Holmes, but I don't know that I ever knew a more workmanlike one than that. We're not jealous of you at Scotland Yard. No, sir, we are very proud of you, and if you come down to-morrow there's not a man, from the oldest inspector to the youngest constable, who wouldn't be glad to shake you by the hand." (SIXN)

99.   *Contradiction is useful.*

Dr. Watson states, "Not for the first time in our long career together I realised it was Holmes's contradictory nature, his Celtic insight that faith in reason cannot be absolute, which was and remains the engine propelling him so swiftly and inexorably along the path from mortal to myth." (Symonds, Codex 148)

100.   *The prospect of Watson's death does not sit well with Holmes.*

Holmes panics when Watson is shot (3GAR). He grows sentimental when Watson asks him to write his epitaph (Symonds, Codex 35).

101.   *Sherlock takes great pride in saving lives.*

"Your life is not your own. Keep your hands off it," he tells the unfortunate Eugenia Ronder (VEIL) and is proud when the brave woman takes his advice.

102. *Irene Adler affects Sherlock more than he lets on.*

She tells him, "You are damaged, delusional, and believe in a higher power; in your case, it's yourself." He does not retaliate – given he is Mr. Punchline who will "outlive God trying to have the last word", it seems a little strange. But then, he does win, in the end...and rescues the damsel, too. (Sherlock: ASIB)

103. *Moriarty is pretty much the perfect villain; he does not get his hands dirty.*

How would you build a case against someone who never performed the act of crime himself? Crime, as we know, has two elements – the *mens rea*, or the guilty intent, and the *actus reus*, or the act itself. Moriarty, the Consulting Criminal, assists the parties with *mens rea* by giving them ideas and plans for the execution of the *actus reus*. He remains "above it all". (Sherlock: TGG) In one instance, he nearly gets Dr. Watson to act as Sherlock Holmes' assassin (Jaynes)!

104. *Mycroft is the guide, the teacher, while Sherlock is the hero, the pupil.*

It appears that from his young days, Sherlock has been delegated the hero's role. He is the one that embarks on quests. When his brother is in danger, Sherlock comes to the rescue, suppressing his emotions so he can aid his brother better. (Lane, Black Ice 50) It has been pointed out to Sherlock, "...you have an older sibling who you admire greatly and your energy springs from a desire to keep pace with him." (Murthy 70)

105. **_You cannot rely on luck._**

"Luck is an offensive, abhorrent concept. The idea that there is a force in the universe tilting events in your favour or against it is ridiculous. Idiots rely on luck," Holmes snaps at Watson (Elementary: Lesser Evils).

106. **_People are afraid of what they do not understand._**

So explains Jonathan Kent to his young son Clark, explaining why he needs to keep his secret (Man of Steel). This is especially true of a genius like Sherlock – some police officers refer to him as "freak" and "psychopath" (Sherlock). Even Stamford, who can be thanked for bringing together the legendary pair of Sherlock Holmes and John Watson in STUD, remarks on the odd nature of Sherlock and is wary of him.

107. *Sherlock Holmes can fight monsters, too, even if they are family.*

Possibly a work of fiction, for I do not know of another instance where brother Thorpe appears – but Holmes shoots his brother to save the life of his friend Dr. Watson (<u>Sherlock Holmes 2010</u>).

108. *Sherlock does not believe in love...or does he?*

"I imagine John Watson thinks love's a mystery to me, but the chemistry is incredibly simple and very destructive," he says to Irene (<u>Sherlock: ASIB</u>). "Love is a much more vicious motivator," he remarks to a serial killer. (Sherlock: ASIP)

109. *Sometimes, you need to take the winding roads to get to your destination.*

Not to advocate illegal activities of any sort (as a lawyer, I am sworn to protect the letter and spirit of the law, anyway) – but Holmes did not always play by the rules, did he? The burglary at Milverton's house (CHAS) or the one at Baron Gruner's (ILLU)

– while not legal, were, nonetheless, morally right to the extent they were undertaken for protection of innocents.

110. *Holmes is not materialistic.*

He is happy in his Baker Street rooms for which he pays "princely sums" (DYIN) to make up for his eccentricities and he says, "My professional charges are upon a fixed scale. I do not vary them, save when I remit them altogether." (THOR) Though, in good humour, he extracts a fair amount from the Duke in PRIO.

111. *Sherlock Holmes never was, and never could be, a fraud or a fake – no matter what anyone says.*

John believes in him. I believe in him. Millions of fans around the world believe in him. (#BelieveinSherlock). It would have been impossible for him to have faked it for one hundred and sixty years.

112. *Sherlock Holmes is almost indefinable.*

However, King and Klinger seem to have come really close to a perfect description, "...a modern-day knight errant; a man whose passion for righting wrongs is mistaken for a cold intellectual curiosity; a tortured hero with but a single friend; a man who never lived "and so can never die," who is more alive today than any other resident of the Victorian Age, including Victoria herself." (King introduction)

113. *Do not let your brain atrophy.*

"Of all ruins that of a noble mind is the most deplorable," Dr. Watson says (DYIN).

114. *Reserve judgment until you have gathered enough information; your first impression may not be accurate.*

Appearances can be deceiving. Holmes explains, "It is of the first importance ... not to allow your judgment to be biased by personal qualities. ... The emotional qualities are antagonistic to clear reasoning. I assure you that the most winning woman I ever knew was hanged for poisoning three little children for their insurance-money, and the most repellent man of my acquaintance is a philanthropist who has spent nearly a quarter of a million upon the London poor." (SIGN)

115. *It is difficult to distinguish the ordinary.*

"Singularity is almost invariably a clue. The more featureless and commonplace a crime is, the more difficult it is to bring it home," Sherlock states (BOSC).

116. *Sherlock Holmes owes his fame to John Watson.*

He confesses, "And here it is that I miss my Watson. By cunning questions and ejaculations of wonder he could elevate my simple art, which is but systematized common sense, into a prodigy. When I tell my own story I have no such aid." (BLAN)

117. *Sherlock Holmes has a soft-corner for dogs.*

"Dogs do not make mistakes," he says (SHOS). His opinion of Toby (SIGN) is higher than that of a lot of policemen, and he remarks, "That the dog should die was after the beautiful, faithful nature of dogs." (LION) He even has a canine avatar (Sherlock Undercover Dog).

118. *Ethics and morality are the basis of society – though fluid.*

Holmes remarks, at the plight of the unfortunate Professor, "When one tries to rise above Nature one is liable to fall below it. The highest type of man may revert to the animal if he leaves the straight road of destiny." (CREE) It is slightly unlike him, for he is man of scientific appetite, and progressive in nature. Perhaps the failed experiment jarred him.

119. ***The only limits are ethics and law and both these things can be very flexible.***

The words of Dr. Jacqui Stapleton (Sherlock: THB) on her experiments. Ethics and law are both social constructs, and change as society changes. What was ethical yesterday may be unethical today – what point of reference do we use in such situations? Would Sherlock know?

120. ***It was worth a wound; it was worth many wounds.***

Probably my favourite scene in the entire canon – Holmes' concern for his companion when he is shot: Dr. Watson writes, "It was worth a wound; it was worth many wounds; to know the depth of loyalty and love which lay behind that cold mask. The clear, hard eyes were dimmed for a moment, and the firm lips were shaking. For the one and only time I caught a glimpse of a great heart as well as of a great brain.

All my years of humble but single-minded service culminated in that moment of revelation." (3GAR)

121. *There is no substitute for diligence.*

"They say that genius is an infinite capacity for taking pains...It is a very bad definition, but it does apply to detective work," says Holmes (STUD).

122. *John Watson is an ideal companion.*

Holmes agrees, "A confederate who foresees your conclusions and course of action is always dangerous, but one to whom each development comes as a perpetual surprise, and to whom the future is always a closed book, is indeed an ideal helpmate." (BLAN)

123. *Inconsistency should raise your alarms.*

Follow Sherlock Holmes when he says, "We must look for consistency. Where there is a want of it we must suspect deception." (THOR)

124. *Come at once if convenient — if inconvenient come all the same.*

Presumptuous, is it not? And yet Dr. Watson puts up with it (CREE, Sherlock: ASIP). Why? A rather irreverent (though highly entertaining) explanation is provided in the play <u>Broken Holmes</u>. (I apologise, but I should not give out spoilers for the play – I will just say that it is brilliant.)

125. *It is simpler to deal direct.*

As always, Sherlock gets straight to the point (SUSS). Mystery at both ends of a case is too much work. (<u>Sherlock: ASIP</u>). That is how he convinces Wu to teach him *T'ai chi ch'uan* (Lane, <u>Snake Bite</u> 36)

126. *Even the great Sherlock Holmes gets homesick.*

Dr. Watson notes, "My friend's temper had not improved since he had been deprived of the congenial surroundings of Baker Street. Without his scrap-books, his chemicals, and his homely untidiness, he was an uncomfortable man." (3STU)

127. *Evidence needs to be examined carefully.*

"Circumstantial evidence is a very tricky thing ... It may seem to point very straight to one thing, but if you shift your own point of view a little, you may find it pointing in an equally uncompromising manner to something entirely different," says Holmes (BOSC).

128. **Relativity is a fact.**

"Everything in this world is relative, my dear Watson." (DYIN) Note how he refuses to leave home for anything less than an eight and yet, plays Christmas music for his house-guests (Sherlock: ASIB) and even ventures to find a snowman for a little girl for Christmas (Ruffle 11).

129. **Twist your theories to fit the fact; do not twist the facts to fit your theories.**

Remember Sherlock's words, "It is impossible as I state it, and therefore I must in some respect have stated it wrong." (PRIO) Remember how he snaps at Detective Inspector Dimmock (Sherlock: TBB), "It is *one* explanation of *some* of the facts!"

130. **If you are true to Sherlock Holmes, he will take you to great heights.**

Is Jeremy Brett not immortalised for his portrayal of Sherlock Holmes? Did the BBC Sherlock not make a star of Benedict Cumberbatch? (Porter) Did Sherlock Holmes not fling Robert Downey Jr to fame? How about Basil Rathbone, Peter Cushing, Jonny Lee Miller? Let me confess – I had not heard of most of these actors before they played Sherlock Holmes. Once they did, however, their other works came to light as well. While Jeremy Brett and Edward Hardwicke made a fantastic Holmes-Watson duo, personally, I think Benedict Cumberbatch and Martin Freeman are the best Sherlock-John team of all – they are modern, spectacular, magnificent! (Yes, I can envision almost everyone a decade (or more) above my age rolling their eyes here.) Look at them now: Benedict Cumberbatch is probably the most talked-about actor in the world at this moment, closely followed by Martin Freeman. Both remain dedicated to Sherlock. I hope and pray they always will.

131. *Sherlock does not particularly admire the gentry.*

He remarks, "This looks like one of those unwelcome social summonses which call upon a man either to be bored or to lie." (NOBL) He turns up in Buckingham Palace in a sheet (Sherlock: ASIB).

132. *Ground yourself in reality first.*

As Sherlock says, "I fear that if the matter is beyond humanity it is certainly beyond me. Yet we must exhaust all natural explanations before we fall back upon such a theory as this." (DEVI)

133. *Unless you have your very own Watson to take care of you, keep your experiments sane and safe.*

John shoots a murderer to save Sherlock (<u>Sherlock: ASIP</u>). Watson pulls Holmes out from a roomful of poisonous smoke before Holmes manages to poison them both (DEVI).

134. *Sherlock Holmes cannot stand dishonourable men.*

The intensity of his reaction to Charles Augustus Milverton reveals it all as he cries to Watson, "I have said that he is the worst man in London, and I would ask you how could one compare the ruffian, who in hot blood bludgeons his mate, with this man, who methodically and at his leisure tortures the soul and wrings the nerves in order to add to his already swollen money-bags?" (CHAS) I can agree with him here – Milverton is certainly the most despicable villain our heroes have encountered.

135. *It is not only the brain attic which needs spring-cleaning – your actual room does, too.*

"An anomaly which often struck me in the character of my friend Sherlock Holmes was that, although in his methods of thought he was the neatest and most methodical of mankind, and although he also affected a certain quiet primness of dress, he was none the less in his personal habits one of the most untidy men that ever drove a fellow-lodger to distraction," Dr. Watson complains (MUSG).

136. *Falling is just like flying, except there is a more permanent destination.*

I could not resist – this is just too cool. Another of Jim Moriarty's gems (Sherlock: TRF) – is he not the scariest and most spectacular criminal ever? The Napoleon of crime – the spider at the centre of his web, indeed.

137. *Passion and genius come at a price, because when there is nothing to direct your passion or genius at, life seems dull, irrelevant.*

Sherlock paid it. You feel your heart twitch in sympathy (though he is effectively wishing for crime to occur) when he laments, "I cannot live without brain-work. What else is there to live for? Stand at the window here. Was ever such a dreary, dismal, unprofitable world? See how the yellow fog swirls down the street and drifts across the dun-coloured houses. What could be more hopelessly prosaic and material? What is the use of having powers, Doctor, when one has no field upon which to exert them? Crime is commonplace, existence is commonplace, and no qualities save those which are commonplace have any function upon earth." (SIGN)

138. ***The deduction of religion by Sherlock Holmes is at once strange and interesting.***

"There is nothing in which deduction is so necessary as in religion...It can be built up as an exact science by the reasoner. Our highest assurance of the goodness of Providence seems to me to rest in the flowers. All other things, our powers our desires, our food, are all really necessary for our existence in the first instance. But this rose is an extra. Its smell and its colour are an embellishment of life, not a condition of it. It is only goodness which gives extras, and so I say again that we have much to hope from the flowers." (NAVA)

139. ***Not everyone is capable of understanding or admiring genius.***

This is why John Watson assumes his significant role. He understands, admires and supports. He provides the stability that a genius requires. He defends, "I have usually found that there was method in his madness." (REIG) Sometimes, though, even the good doctor is in over his head - "What? You can't hear the thunder and lightning?" Holmes asks him, playing music which the doctor describes as "the tumult of sound now assaulting my ears". (Gillman, Birchwood)

140. ***Holmes knows that he is neither inerrant nor infallible.***

He requests Watson to be his control when he says, "If it should ever strike you that I am getting a little over-confident in my powers, or giving less pains to a case than it deserves, kindly whisper 'Norbury' in my ear, and I shall be infinitely obliged to you." (YELL) Well, I beg to differ, but then, that is fandom for you.

141. *For someone with no knowledge of philosophy, Sherlock certainly has a lot of little nuggets.*

For example, take this, "Before turning to those moral and mental aspects of the matter which present the greatest difficulties, let the inquirer begin by mastering more elementary problems." (STUD)

142. *Knowledge is power.*

Holmes remarks, "In my profession all sorts of odd knowledge comes useful, and this room of yours is a storehouse of it." (3GAR)

143. *Sherlock Holmes respects Moriarty – he enjoys the "game" as much as the evil genius does.*

Though, even as he bemoans the sloth of London criminals and the unoriginality of the criminal classes subsequent to the demise of Professor Moriarty (NORW), he never strays from the path of justice. How easy it would be for a prodigious, manically-active mind like his to be led astray, just to find some peace (SIGN, WIST). But he remains "on the side of the angels" (Sherlock: TRF), even to his detriment.

144. *Health advice from Sherlock Holmes is not really something to take seriously.*

Really, not eating for days because apparently, digestion hinders brain-work? But, there is nothing wrong with – "There can be no question, my dear Watson, of the value of exercise before breakfast." (BLAC) – even if the said exercise did consist of harpooning a dead pig.

145. *All fairy tales need a good old-fashioned villain.*

True enough, Mr. Jim Moriarty (Sherlock: TRF) and we are grateful for your existence, for you gave Sherlock the best puzzles to solve, and your darkness made him shine like an angel. What is a hero without an evil mastermind to defeat?

146. *Sherlock Holmes takes his work very, very seriously.*

"It is not so impossible, however, that a man should possess all knowledge which is likely to be useful to him in his work, and this, I have endeavoured in my case to do," he confesses (FIVE). The amount of time and energy taken to learn so much would be humongous.

147. *Holmes did not really approve of his Watson going away.*

"Holmes spoke seldom about my domestic arrangements. He had been abroad at the time of my wedding and it had occurred to me then that it might not have been entirely a coincidence. It would be unfair to say that the entire subject of my marriage was forbidden, but there was an unspoken agreement that we would not discuss it at any length. My happiness and contentment were evident to Holmes, and he was generous enough not to begrudge it," Watson notes (Horowitz 8). And, of course, we should not forget the original conversation, as narrated by Dr. Watson (SIGN):

> "Well, and there is the end of our little drama," I remarked, after we had set some time smoking in silence. "I fear that it may be the last investigation in which I shall have the chance of studying your methods. Miss Morstan has done me the honour to accept me as a husband in prospective."

He gave a most dismal groan. "I feared as much," said he. "I really cannot congratulate you."

I was a little hurt. "Have you any reason to be dissatisfied with my choice?" I asked.

"Not at all. I think she is one of the most charming young ladies I ever met, and might have been most useful in such work as we have been doing. She had a decided genius that way: witness the way in which she preserved that Agra plan from all the other papers of her father. But love is an emotional thing, and whatever is emotional is opposed to that true cold reason which I place above all things. I should never marry myself, lest I bias my judgment."

148. *It is possible that Sherlock's early life was not particularly happy.*

There has been much speculation on his early life. Some depictions of his early life narrate adventures and romantic tragedies (Young Sherlock Holmes) while others delve into darker events concerning his parents (The Seven-Per-Cent Solution).

149. *University was probably not fun for Sherlock, either.*

Not if he went to college with the likes of Sebastian Wilkes (Sherlock: TBB), though Victor Trevor (GLOR) and Reginald Musgrave (MUSG) seem decent enough.

150. *Sherlock and John are birds of a feather.*

"I know, my dear Watson, that you share my love of all that is bizarre and outside the conventions and humdrum routine of everyday life," Holmes says (REDH).

151. *Dealing with evil is not all fun and games; you pay a price, too.*

"Nobody knew evil like Holmes, but there are some evils that it is better not to know, and he could not enjoy even the rewards of his success without being reminded of the dark places to which it had taken him," says Dr. Watson (Horowitz 293).

152. ***Mrs. Hudson loves her boys.***

What landlady would put up with the two madmen, otherwise? And her boys love her. "Mrs. Hudson leave Baker Street? England would fall," Sherlock says.

153. ***Irene Adler is quite taken with Sherlock Holmes.***

She is "SHERLOCKED", after all (Sherlock: ASIB) and she flirts with him. After all, brainy is the new sexy. In Elementary, she is in love with him – and even more interestingly, she is Moriarty.

154. ***Molly Hooper worships Sherlock Holmes.***

And Sherlock Holmes trusts her in return – not something you hear from Sherlock often, "You do matter. You have always mattered and I have always trusted you." (Sherlock: TRF)

155. ***Mycroft is very protective of his younger brother.***

He knows his sibling's vulnerabilities; facts which Sherlock himself would disregard. "All lives end. All hearts are broken. Caring is not an advantage, Sherlock," he counsels, or attempts to console a bereaved Sherlock (Sherlock: ASIB). It seems to be the Holmes family motto. And yet, Mycroft actually worries about his brother (constantly) and goes to insane lengths to vet his contacts (Sherlock: ASIP).

156. ***Moriarty loves to play with Sherlock Holmes.***

"I like to watch you dance," Jim Moriarty tells Sherlock through a stolen voice. "I have enjoyed this,; this little game of ours..." he says upon their first (well, second) meeting (Sherlock: TGG).

157. ***Detective Inspector Lestrade admires Sherlock Holmes.***

On being asked why he puts up with the eccentric detective, he confesses, "Because Sherlock Holmes is a great man – and one day, if we are very, very lucky, he might even be a good one." (Sherlock: ASIP) Well, the Detective Inspector's wish has come true.

158. ***The greatest mystery of all is why we are so enamoured of Sherlock Holmes – but each of us has a perfectly justified reason.***

Food for thought: "Why on earth the constant need to push Holmes onto an ever-gullible public? You'd have thought everyone would be sick to death of him by now, but there's a never-ending stream of it and it's only gotten worse of late. Every damn Tom,

Dick, and Harry is dreaming up some new madcap scheme or other to do with Holmes and Watson. There are those dreadful big-budget Hollywood films, the damn TV series, seemingly multiple ones; books and audio books and bloody e-books, all coming out of our bloody ears; and that's not counting those violent bloody video games and all those weird comic books intended for illiterate adults. For the life of me, I can't imagine what it is everyone hopes to achieve with it all. And I absolutely dread to think where it's all going to end. They should just bloody well leave well enough alone and stick with the Canon, plain and simple; surely that should be good enough? I know none of it's still in copyright, but is that any reason for everyone to keep on taking a bite out of the old beekeeping bugger?" (Broadbent 29)

159. *Dr. Watson is in awe of Sherlock Holmes.*

"I had no idea that such individuals exist outside of stories," he says (STUD).

160. *We adore Sherlock Holmes, too, ad infinitum.*

I do not need to explain that, do I?

The Holmes Sutra: Part II

The Holmes Mania Quotient Test

Sherlock Holmes is, quite possibly, the most popular detective in the world. What is it that makes him so attractive? It has been more than a century since Sherlock Holmes first appeared in Beeton's Christmas Annual in 1887, and yet, to this day, he remains as popular as ever. While some of the current mania could possibly be attributed to Sherlock, Elementary and Sherlock Holmes and Sherlock Holmes: Game – Sherlock Holmes has never really been out of the public eye since he rose to fame at the end of the nineteenth century. Most admirers (well, most that I have come across, anyway) of Sherlock Holmes appear to be people who were introduced to him during their pre-teen/teenage years, and have remained captivated for life.

It is a mystery worthy of Sherlock himself – why is he as addictive to the masses as his drug of choice? Is it because he stimulates our minds? Or is it because he appeals at once to the logical and the dramatic sides of us?

A friend of mine once remarked, "You can love him, you can hate him – but you cannot ignore Sherlock Holmes." How true. He creeps up on you and holds you captive, and you are too fascinated to care.

Once you are his, you belong to him for life. Happily ever after.

The addiction may not be explainable, but the symptoms are easy to recognise. I call it "Holmes Mania". If you are actually reading this, you probably suffer from some form of Holmes Mania.

Here comes a little test for your Holmes Mania Quotient (HMQ) – based on your HMQ score, your diagnosis will be determined. I have come up with five basic conditions:

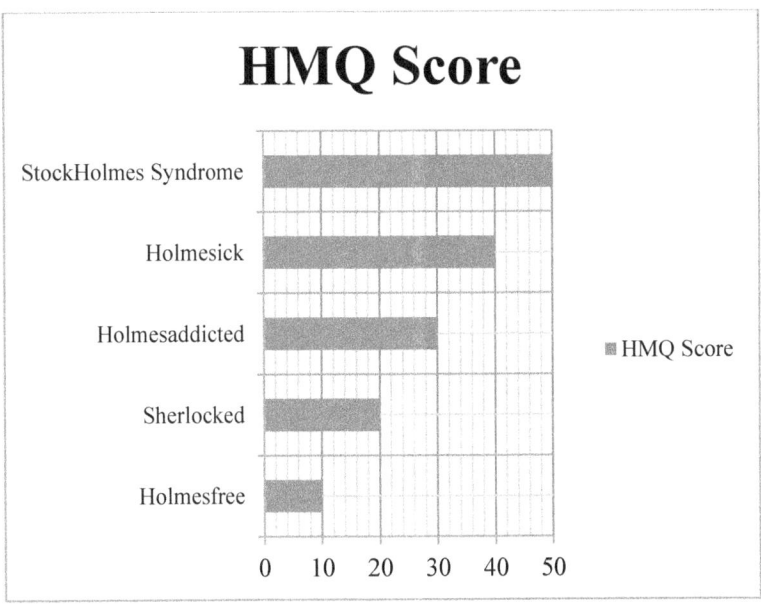

So, are you ready to record your HMQ score?

Grab a pencil and put a bookmark on the following page. It contains your HMQ score-sheet; you will have to keep turning back to put down your answers.

Once you have answered all ten questions, you will find the score chart. Based on your answers, put down your score for each question, and then calculate the total.

I should mention here that Holmes Mania is progressive in nature – it develops in stages.

The total is your HMQ score. Find your Holmes Mania.

Question No.	Your Answer	Your HMQ Score
(A)		
(B)		
(C)		
(D)		
(E)		
(F)		
(G)		
(H)		
(I)		
(J)		

Your Total HMQ Score: _____

Pen/pencil? Bookmark?

Take a deep breath. Are you ready?

Here we go:

(A) **Where is the real 221B, Baker Street located?**

    1)   At the Sherlock Holmes Museum, Baker Street

    2)   In your head

    3)   Above Speedy's Cafe

    4)   Somewhere in London

    5)   Outside the Baker Street Tube Station

    6)   No idea

(B) **Who is your favourite Holmes?**

    1)   Benedict Cumberbatch

    2)   Jonny Lee Miller

    3)   Robert Downey Junior

    4)   Jeremy Brett

    5)   Peter Cushing

    6)   Basil Rathbone

    7)   All of them

    8)   The one in your head

    9)   Er…who are these people?

(C) **The Art of Observation: You are given a photograph of a sheet of paper. What do you see?**

1) It's just a bit of paper.

2) You can read enough text to know what document it is.

3) You know what type of pen was used to sign it.

4) You can tell what instrument was used to cut the paper.

5) You can see the surroundings of the photograph.

6) You know what paper stock that is as well.

(D) **The Science of Deduction: You are given a painting of the silhouette of a soldier with a sandy, war-zone background. What can you deduce from the picture?**

1) What a pretty picture!

2) Hey, look, the artist signed it!

3) You can tell you a bit about the location of the silhouette.

4) You know who I am talking about.

5) You can tell the entire history of this person, including the model of the gun they are carrying.

6) Who knows? Who cares?

(E) **If Sherlock Holmes were to appear in corporeal form in your room at this very instant, what would you do?**

1) Wonder who the pale, thin, strange-looking guy is.

2) Run away screaming once you have recovered from your fainting spell.

3) Shake hands with him, then pull out your phone and call your psychiatrist.

4) Timidly ask for an autograph and a photograph.

5) Ask him how he is enjoying his trip to your place and whether John and Mycroft would be joining him soon, then offer to take him sight-seeing.

6) You don't see anybody.

(F) **Sherlockiana: You have read:**

1) The Canon

2) The Canon and a few pastiches that came highly recommended

3) The Canon, a few pastiches and some articles

4) The Canon, pastiches, comics, scripts, articles in papers/journals

5) The Canon, pastiches, comics, articles in papers/journals, anything remotely related to Sherlock Holmes that you can find, including random fan-fiction online

6) You have no idea what we are talking about

(G) **A friend or someone you care about is miffed with you – because you said/did something they did not agree with and came across as insensitive. Now you need their help and they remain stubbornly silent, waiting for you to apologise first. Your reaction:**

1) You have no idea they are miffed with you

2) You apologise and do something nice for them

3) You sulk and then do it yourself

4) You ask, "Not good?"

5) You tell them, "Caring is not an advantage."

6) You say, "Not much cop, this caring lark."

(H) **You have not had much work in the past few days. How do you feel?**

1) You are quite happy and relaxed, enjoying the peace

2) It is nice for a day, but then you start getting bored

3) Bored. Bored. BORED!

4) You are bored and irritable and shouting at everyone nearby

5) You are turning your home upside down looking for a distraction, or preferably, and addictive substance

6) You are shooting at walls

(I)   You collect Holmesian artefacts:

1) You have some books

2) You have some gifts and prizes

3) You have amassed a collection of Sherlockian things from all over the world as souvenirs during your travel

4) You keep an eye out for interesting artefacts and buy them as soon as you can

5) Your family is threatening to throw you out because your Holmesian stuff is spilling out of everywhere

6) Huh, what?

(J)   If you could be anyone you wanted to be, including fictional or historical characters, who would you be?

1) Arthur Conan Doyle

2) Mycroft Holmes

3) Sherlock Holmes

4) John Watson

5) Someone related to/inspired by Sherlock Holmes

6) Someone who has no nexus with Sherlock Holmes, and is as dissimilar to him as chalk and cheese

Now that you have successfully completed the test, take note of your scores for each question:

Question No.	Answer	Score
(A)	1	3
	2	5
	3	2
	4	1
	5	4
	6	0
(B)	1	2
	2 or 3	1
	4, 5 or 6	3
	7	4
	8	5
	9	0
(C)	1	0
	2	1
	3	2
	4	3
	5	4
	6	5
(D)	1	1
	2	2
	3	3
	4	4
	5	5
	6	0
(E)	1	1
	2	2
	3	3
	4	4
	5	5
	6	0

Question No.	Answer	Score
(F)	1	1
	2	2
	3	3
	4	4
	5	5
	6	0
(G)	1	0
	2	1
	3	2
	4	3
	5	4
	6	5
(H)	1	0
	2	1
	3	2
	4	3
	5	4
	6	5
(I)	1	1
	2	2
	3	3
	4	4
	5	5
	6	0
(J)	1	2
	2	3
	3	4
	4	5
	5	1
	6	0

Now, add up and match your total score:

Your HMQ Score	Your Holmes Mania
0-10	Holmesfree
11-20	Sherlocked
21-30	Holmesaddicted
31-40	Holmesick
41-50	StockHolmes Syndrome

You have been diagnosed.

Details of your condition follow:

What does your HMQ score mean?

I. *Holmes Mania Stage 1: Holmesfree*

HMQ Score: 0 to 10

You range from having no clue about the detective to having a mild appreciation for the man. Sherlock has nil to negligible impact or influence on you.

You are probably safe.

For now.

II. *Holmes Mania Stage 2: Sherlocked*

HMQ Score: 11 to 20

Irene Adler's term (Sherlock: ASIP) – and of course, you already know this. You harbour a healthy dose of adoration for our dear consulting detective.

You are probably a relatively new entry into the world of Sherlock Holmes.

By "normal" standards, this is probably the best stage of Holmes Mania.

III. *Holmes Mania Stage 3: Holmesaddicted*

HMQ Score: 21-30

The moment you protest, "I am not an addict!" you are doomed. You adore Sherlock Holmes in all forms, and you just can't get enough.

You have probably set your Google Alerts (or whatever search engine you use) to notify you when "Sherlock" or "Sherlock Holmes" pops up - and possibly, you have set this alert for each of the Holmesian characters and each of the Holmesian media you have taken a liking to.

Could be dangerous.

IV.   *Holmes Mania Stage 4: Holmesick*

HMQ Score: 31-40

You suffer from a psychological condition where the patient complains of mental trauma and quite often, also suffers from associated psychosomatic aches, when completely deprived of the company of Sherlock Holmes in any form for an extended period of time.

It may be noted that the illness may manifest regardless of whether the abstinence is voluntary or forced. Oh dear!

V.   *Holmes Mania Stage 5: StockHolmes Syndrome*

HMQ Score: 41-50

You suffer from a psychological condition where the patient exhibits maniacal hoarding tendencies towards any media, object or discussion referring to, or in connection with Sherlock Holmes. Early symptoms include being Sherlocked, obsessive acquisition of Holmesian goods and incessant quoting of dialogues from various Holmesian media during conversations, and you have chronologically passed through the previous stages.

Dear Sherlockian, it is probably time for you to seek help. This is a bit not good.

A Cure...?

How is your Holmes Mania affecting your life? Are you enjoying it? Are you happy? If you are, then why would you even want a cure?

The possibility of a cure…well, as I have said before, deriving the principle from a t-shirt slogan ("The best cure for a hangover is to stay drunk.")

If you are Holmesfree, then you are least bothered.

If you are Sherlocked, you are likely to be quite happy – and once season 3 comes through, you'll be even happier.

If you are Holmesaddicted, well – so long as you are high on Holmes, and can still be a high-functioning member of the society, how does it matter?

If you are Holmesick, well, do speak to your doctors and employers and try and get them to recognise Holmesickness as a legitimate cause for availing sick-leave. After all, the only cure is to go to your Holmes.

If you suffer from StockHolmes Syndrome, you are probably happier and more content that 90% of the world's population. If you are so happy, there is no reason for you to seek a cure. If you are unhappy, book an appointment with your therapist.

The game is afoot.

Canon Abbreviations

The conventional abbreviations (as listed below) were devised by Jay Finley Christ and use four letters.

S. No.	Abbreviation	Story
1.	ABBE	The Adventure of the Abbey Grange
2.	BERY	The Adventure of the Beryl Coronet
3.	BLAC	The Adventure of Black Peter
4.	BLAN	The Adventure of the Blanched Soldier
5.	BLUE	The Adventure of the Blue Carbuncle
6.	BOSC	The Boscombe Valley Mystery
7.	BRUC	The Adventure of the Bruce-Partington Plans
8.	CARD	The Adventure of the Cardboard Box
9.	CHAS	The Adventure of Charles Augustus Milverton

S. No.	Abbreviation	Story
10.	COPP	The Adventure of the Copper Beeches
11.	CREE	The Adventure of the Creeping Man
12.	CROO	The Adventure of the Crooked Man
13.	DANC	The Adventure of the Dancing Men
14.	DEVI	The Adventure of the Devil's Foot
15.	DYIN	The Adventure of the Dying Detective
16.	EMPT	The Adventure of the Empty House
17.	ENGR	The Adventure of the Engineer's Thumb
18.	FINA	The Final Problem
19.	FIVE	The Five Orange Pips
20.	GLOR	The Gloria Scott
21.	GOLD	The Adventure of the Golden Pince-nez
22.	GREE	The Greek Interpreter

S. No.	Abbreviation	Story
23.	HOUN	The Hound of the Baskervilles
24.	IDEN	A Case of Identity
25.	ILLU	The Adventure of the Illustrious Client
26.	LADY	The Disappearance of Lady Frances Carfax
27.	LAST	His Last Bow
28.	LION	The Adventure of the Lion's Mane
29.	MAZA	The Adventure of the Mazarin Stone
30.	MISS	The Adventure of the Missing Three-Quarter
31.	MUSG	The Musgrave Ritual
32.	NAVA	The Naval Treaty
33.	NOBL	The Adventure of the Noble Bachelor
34.	NORW	The Adventure of the Norwood Builder

S. No.	Abbreviation	Story
35.	PRIO	The Adventure of the Priory School
36.	REDC	The Adventure of the Red Circle
37.	REDH	The Red-Headed League
38.	REIG	The Reigate Squires
39.	RESI	The Resident Patient
40.	RETI	The Adventure of the Retired Colourman
41.	SCAN	A Scandal in Bohemia
42.	SECO	The Adventure of the Second Stain
43.	SHOS	The Adventure of Shoscombe Old Place
44.	SIGN	The Sign of the Four
45.	SILV	Silver Blaze
46.	SIXN	The Adventure of the Six Napoleons
47.	SOLI	The Adventure of the Solitary Cyclist

S. No.	Abbreviation	Story
48.	SPEC	The Adventure of the Speckled Band
49.	STOC	The Stockbroker's Clerk
50.	STUD	A Study in Scarlet
51.	SUSS	The Adventure of the Sussex Vampire
52.	THOR	The Problem of Thor Bridge
53.	3GAB	The Adventure of the Three Gables
54.	3GAR	The Adventure of the Three Garridebs
55.	3STU	The Adventure of the Three Students
56.	TWIS	The Man with the Twisted Lip
57.	VALL	The Valley of Fear
58.	VEIL	The Adventure of the Veiled Lodger
59.	WIST	The Adventure of the Wisteria Lodge
60.	YELL	The Yellow Face

Bibliography

Literature

1. Adams, Guy. Sherlock: The Casebook. Wemding: BBC Books, 2013.

2. Bangs, John Kendrick. Raffles Holmes & Company. N.p.: Wildside Press, 2003.

3. Baring-Gould, William S. Sherlock Holmes of Baker Street: A Life of the World's First Consulting Detective. New York: Random House, 1995.

4. Broadbent, Tony. As to "An Exact Knowledge of London". Ed. King, Laurie R. and Leslie S. Klinger. A Study in Sherlock. New York: Bantam Books, 2011.

5. Christ, Jay Finley. An Irregular Guide to Sherlock Holmes of Baker Street. New York: Argus Books, 1947.

6. Corey, Daniel. Moriarty: The Lazarus Tree. Berkeley: Dangerkatt Creative Studio, 2011.

7. Cosson, M.J. and Murray Shaw. On the Case with Holmes and Watson #7: Sherlock Holmes and the Red Headed League. Minneapolis: Lerner Publishing Group, 2012.

8. Cosson, M.J. and Murray Shaw. On the Case with Holmes and Watson #14: Sherlock Holmes and the Gloria Scott. Minneapolis: Lerner Publishing Group, 2012.

9. Descartes, René. Principles of Philosophy. Trans. Valentine Rodger Miller and Resse P. Miller. Dordrecht: Kluwer Academic Publishers, 1991.

10. Dexter, Colin. A Case of Mis-identity. Privately printed for the Sherlock Holmes Society of London, 1998.

11. Doyle, Steven and David A Crowder. Sherlock Holmes for Dummies. Indianapolis: Wiley Publishing Inc., 2010.

12. Duncan, Alistair. Close to Holmes. London: MX Publishing, 2009.

13. Ed. Ellis, Bob and Guy Marriott. I Proceeded to Portsmouth. The Sherlock Holmes Society of London, 2008.

14. Ed. Emecz, Steve. Hannah Rogers. <u>The Art of Deduction: A Sherlock Holmes Collection</u>. London: MX Publishing, 2013.

15. Estleman, Loren D. Introduction. <u>Sherlock Holmes: The Complete Novels Stories</u>. Vol. 1&2. By Sir Arthur Conan Doyle. New York: Bantam Classics, 2003.

16. Fields, L.A. <u>My Dear Watson</u>. (e-book) New Jersey: Lethe Press, 2013.

17. Foad, Ross K. <u>Holmes in Time for Christmas</u>. London: MX Publishing, 2013.

18. Foad, Ross K. <u>The Story and Scripts Behind No Place Like Holmes</u>. London: MX Publishing, 2013.

19. Ed. Hardy-Gould, Janet. <u>Sherlock Holmes: The Emerald Crown</u>. Shanghai: Oxford University Press, 2010.

20. Huw-J. <u>The Young Sherlock Holmes Adventures</u>. London: Markosia Enterprises Limited, 2010.

21. Jaynes, Roger. <u>Sherlock Holmes: A Duel with The Devil</u>. London: Linford Leicester, 2004.

22. Kasius, Jennifer. Sherlock Holmes: The Essential Mysteries in One Sitting. Philadelphia: Running Press, 2013.

23. Ed. King, Laurie R. and Leslie S. Klinger. A Study in Sherlock. New York: Bantam Books, 2011.

24. Klinger, Leslie. Preface. The New Annotated Sherlock Holmes: The Complete Short Stories. Vol. 1&2. By Sir Arthur Conan Doyle. New York: W.W. Norton & Company, 2004.

25. Klinger, Leslie. Preface. The New Annotated Sherlock Holmes: The Novels. Vol. 3. By Sir Arthur Conan Doyle. New York: W.W. Norton & Company, 2004.

26. Konnikova, Maria. Mastermind: How to Think Like Sherlock Holmes. Edinburgh: Canongate Books Limited, 2013.

27. Kuhns, Luke Benjamen. Sherlock Holmes: Studies in Legacy. London: MX Publishing, 2013.

28. Kuhns, Luke Benjamen. Sherlock Holmes & The Case of the Crystal Blue Bottle. London: MX Publishing, 2012.

29. Kuhns, Luke Benjamen. The Untold Adventures of Sherlock Holmes. London: MX Publishing, 2012.

30. Lane, Andrew. Black Ice. Croydon: Macmillan Books, 2011.

31. Lane, Andrew. Death Cloud. Croydon: Macmillan Books, 2010.

32. Lane, Andrew. Fire Storm. Croydon: Macmillan Books, 2011.

33. Lane, Andrew. Red Leech. Croydon: Macmillan Books, 2010.

34. Lane, Andrew. Snake Bite. London: Macmillan Books, 2012.

35. McMullen, Keiran. Sherlock Holmes and the Irish Rebels. London: MX Publishing, 2011.

36. Meyer, Nicholas. The Canary Trainer: From the Memoirs of John H. Watson, M.D. New York: W.W. Norton & Company, 1995.

37. Meyer, Nicholas. The Seven-Per-Cent Solution: Being a Reprint from the Reminiscences of John

H. Watson, M.D. New York: W.W. Norton & Company, 1993.

38. Meyer, Nicholas. The West End Horror: A Posthumous Memoir of John H. Watson, M.D. New York: W.W. Norton & Company, 1994.

39. Murthy, Vasudev (writing as Akira Yamashita). Sherlock Holmes in Japan. Noida: HarperCollins Publishers India, 2013.

40. Newman, Kim. Professor Moriarty: The Hound of the D'Urbervilles. London: Titan Books, 2011.

41. Norbu, Jamyang. The Mandala of Sherlock Holmes: The Adventures of the Great Detective in India and Tibet. New Delhi: HarperCollins, 1999.

42. Orwell, George. 1984. New York: Signet Classic, 1977.

43. Porter, Lynnette. Benedict Cumberbatch, In Transition: An Unauthorised Performance Biography. London: MX Publishing, 2013.

44. Riccardi, Ted. The Lost Years of Sherlock Holmes. Mumbai: Jaico Publishing House, 2013.

45. Ruffle, David and Rikey Austin. Sherlock Holmes and the Missing Snowman. London: MX Publishing, 2012.

46. Sherlock Holmes Society of India. Proceedings of the Pondicherry Lodge. Volume 1 Issue 1. 1 June 2013.

47. Springer, Nancy. The Case of the Missing Marquess. New York: Puffin Books, 2006.

48. Springer, Nancy. The Case of the Left-Handed Lady. New York: Puffin Books, 2007.

49. Springer, Nancy. The Case of the Bizarre Bouquets. New York: Puffin Books, 2008.

50. Springer, Nancy. The Case of the Peculiar Pink Fan. New York: Puffin Books, 2008.

51. Springer, Nancy. The Case of the Cryptic Crinoline. New York: Puffin Books, 2009.

52. Springer, Nancy. The Case of the Gypsy Goodbye. New York: Puffin Books, 2010.

53. Ed. Steiff, Josef. Sherlock Holmes and Philosophy: The Footprints of a Gigantic Mind. Chicago: Open Court Publishing Company, 2013.

54. Stoker, Bram. <u>Dracula</u>. Ed. Paul Negri and Kathy Casey. New York: Dover Publications Inc., 2000.

55. Symonds, Tim. <u>Sherlock Holmes and the Dead Boer at Scotney Castle</u>. ("**Boer**") London: MX Publishing, 2012.

56. Symonds, Tim. <u>Sherlock Holmes and the Case of the Bulgarian Codex</u>. ("**Codex**") London: MX Publishing, 2012.

57. Terjesen, Andrew. <u>What Mycroft Knows that Sherlock Doesn't</u>. Ed. Steiff, Josef. <u>Sherlock Holmes and Philosophy: The Footprints of a Gigantic Mind</u>. Chicago: Open Court Publishing Company, 2013.

58. The Sherlock Holmes Society of London. <u>The Sherlock Holmes Journal</u>. Volume 31 No. 2 (issue 121). Summer 2013.

59. Thomas, Donald. <u>The Execution of Sherlock Holmes</u>. ("**Execution**") Mumbai: Jaico Publishing House, 2013.

60. Thomas, Donald. <u>The New Adventures of Sherlock Holmes: The Case of the Ghosts at Bly</u>. ("**Bly**") Mumbai: Jaico Publishing House, 2013.

Web Resources

61. #BelieveinSherlock. 10 September 2013. <www.believeinsherlock.tumblr.com>

62. Allen, Nick. Sir Arthur Conan Doyle's Sherlock Holmes in A Case of Identity. 17 September 2013. <http://www.telegraph.co.uk/culture/books/bookn ews/10310881/Sir-Arthur-Conan-Doyles-Sherlock-Holmes-in-A-Case-of-Identity.html>

63. Asher-Perrin, Emily. What is the #BelieveinSherlock Movement? And How Did it Get So Widespread So Quickly?. 10 September 2013. <http://www.tor.com/blogs/2012/01/what-is-the-believeinsherlock-movement-and-how-did-it-get-so-widespread-so-quickly>

64. Aurora_swan. Hamish the Invisible Boy. 10 September 2013. <http://archiveofourown.org/works/789278?view_full_work=true>

65. Bond, Aimee and Kimberly Buckley. Sherlock series 3: 10 things we learned from the teaser trailer video. 18 September 2013.

<http://www.mirror.co.uk/tv/tv-previews/sherlock-series-3-10-things-2124800>

66. Bragg, Thomas Glynn. "A Mere Appendix": The Reclaiming and Desexing of Sherlock Holmes. University of Florida, 2004. 15 June 2013. <http://etd.fcla.edu/UF/UFE0002729/bragg_t.pdf>

67. Czech Society of Sherlock Holmes. 10 September 2013. <http://www.sherlockholmes.cz/>

68. Cumberbatchweb. 10 September 2013. <http://www.benedictcumberbatch.co.uk/>

69. Deen, Sarah. BBC unveils new drama preview trailer showcasing Sherlock and Ripper Street. ("**BBC preview**") 17 September 2013. <http://metro.co.uk/2013/09/01/bbc-unveils-new-drama-preview-trailer-showcasing-sherlock-and-ripper-street-3945303/>

70. Die Deutsche Sherlock Holmes Gesellschaft. 10 September 2013. <http://dshc.de/>

71. Ganguly, Jayantika. Understanding Human Doormats. ("**Doormats**") 17 June 2013. < http://www.boloji.com/index.cfm?md=Content&sd=Articles&ArticleID=3201>

72. Ganguly, Jayantika. Understanding BUNDY Souls. ("**BUNDY**") 17 June 2013. < http://www.boloji.com/index.cfm?md=Content&sd=Articles&ArticleID=3213>

73. Ganguly, Jayantika. Understanding Drama Queens. ("Drama Queens") 17 June 2013. < http://www.boloji.com/index.cfm?md=Content&sd=Articles&ArticleID=6850>

74. Hall, Ellie. Everything You NEED To Know About The Sherlock Comic-Con Panel. 17 September 2013. <http://www.buzzfeed.com/ellievhall/everything-you-need-to-know-about-the-sherlock-comic-con-pan>

75. Hamish Watson Holmes. 17 June 2013. <http://ask-hamish-holmes.tumblr.com/>

76. I Hear of Sherlock Everywhere. 10 September 2013. <http://www.ihearofsherlock.com/>

77. Intellectual Parasites Of Diogenes (IPOD) Club. 16 September 2013. <http://www.sherlockian-sherlock.com/diogenes-club.php>

78. Jefferies, Mark. Sir Ian McKellen to play Sherlock Holmes in new movie A Slight Trick Of The Mind. 18 September 2013. <http://www.mirror.co.uk/lifestyle/going-out/film/ian-mckellen-play-sherlock-holmes-2254610>

79. Leloi. Hamish, 10 September 2013. <http://archiveofourown.org/works/938780>

80. Maybe Amanda and OneMillionAndNine. Sustain (or Concerto for the Famished in D Minor). 17 June 2013. <http://archiveofourown.org/works/217671?view_full_work=true>

81. Plaidbaby. Bunnies and Brollies. 17 June 2013. <http://archiveofourown.org/works/414383?view_full_work=true>

82. Punny_Puck. Q Becomes Q. 10 September 2013. <http://archiveofourown.org/works/736437>

83. Q Holmes. Archive of Our Own: Fan-fiction. 15 June 2013. < http://archiveofourown.org/tags/Q%20is%20a%20Holmes/works>

84.   Rector. The Double-First of Mycroft Holmes. 17
      June   2013.
      <http://archiveofourown.org/works/730724?view_
      full_work=true>

85.   Rector. Mycroft Holmes: Master of Secrets. 17
      September   2013.
      <http://archiveofourown.org/works/825789?view_
      full_work=true>

86.   Rector. The Wedding of Cate Adin and Mycroft
      Holmes.   17   September   2013.
      <http://archiveofourown.org/works/928508>

87.   Rector. The Sabbatical of Mycroft Holmes. 17
      September   2013.
      <http://archiveofourown.org/works/938281?view_
      full_work=true>

88.   Rector. The Education of Mycroft Holmes. 17
      September   2013.
      <http://archiveofourown.org/works/
      578920?view_full_work=true>

89.   Rector. Mycroft Holmes: A Terminal Degree. 17
      September   2013.

<http://archiveofourown.org/works/ 579030?view_full_work=true>

90. Rector. Mycroft Holmes and the Trivium Protocol. 17 September 2013. <http://archiveofourown.org/works/ 579043?view_full_work=true>

91. Rector. Mycroft Holmes in Excelsis. 17 September 2013. <http://archiveofourown.org/works/ 634299?view_full_work=true>

92. Scuttlebutt from Spermaceti Press. 16 June 2013. <http://www.sherlocktron.com/scuttle.htm>

93. Sherlock: A Study in Pink ("**ASIP**") Quotes. 10 September 2013. <http://www.imdb.com/title/tt1665071/quotes>

94. Sherlock Holmes News. 17 September 2013. <http://www.sherlocknews.com/>

95. Sherlock Holmes Society of India. 16 June 2013. <http://www.sherlockholmessociety.in>

96. Sherlockian. 16 June 2013. < http://www.sherlockian.net/>

97. Sherlockians: The Fandom That Waited ("**TFTW**"). 10 September 2013. <https://www.facebook.com/...Fandom-That-Waited/491558760909274>

98. Sherlockian Who's Who. 10 September 2013. <http://www.sh-whoswho.com/>

99. Sherlockology. 16 June 2013. < http://www.sherlockology.com/>

100. Sherlockology, Sherlockabilia - The Sherlockology Shop for the Sherlockologist in everyone. 14 June 2013. <http://www.sherlockabilia.com/index.html>

101. Sir Arthur Conan Doyle Literary Estate. 18 September 2013. <http://www.sherlockholmesonline.org/>

102. The Art of Deduction. 16 June 2013 < http://www.artofdeduction.com/holmesian-deduction/>

103. The Baker Street Irregulars ("**BSI**"), The Baker Street Journal: 2014 News. 13 June 2013. <http://www.bakerstreetjournal.com/bsiweekend.html>

104. The Red Circle of Washington DC. 10 September 2013. <http://redcircledc.org/>

105. The Science of Deduction. 16 June 2013. <http://www.thescienceofdeduction.co.uk/>

106. The Sherlock Holmes Museum. 18 September 2013. <http://www.sherlock-holmes.co.uk/>

107. The Sherlock Holmes Society of London. 16 June 2013. ("**SHSL**") <http://www.sherlock-holmes.org.uk/district.php>

108. Watson, John H. The Personal Blog of John H. Watson. ("**Blog**") 16 June 2013. <http://www.johnwatsonblog.co.uk/>

109. White_Noise. The Other Life of Quentin Holmes, Quartermaster (series). 10 September 2013. <http://archiveofourown.org/series/30342>

110. Wikipedia: Schrödinger's Cat. 10 September 2013. <http://en.wikipedia.org/wiki/Schr%C3%B6dinger 's_cat>

Cinematographic resources

111. <u>Broken Holmes</u>. Dir. Robin Johnson. Perf. James Bober, Canavan Connolly. University College London, 20 June 2013.

112. <u>Elementary: Pilot</u>. Dir. Michael Cuesta. Perf. Jonny Lee Miller, Lucy Liu. CBS. 2012.

113. <u>Elementary: While You Were Sleeping</u>. Dir. John David Coles. Perf. Jonny Lee Miller, Lucy Liu. CBS. 2012.

114. <u>Elementary: Child Predator</u>. Dir. Rod Holcomb. Perf. Jonny Lee Miller, Lucy Liu. CBS. 2012.

115. <u>Elementary: The Rat Race</u>. Dir. Rosemary Rodriguez. Perf. Jonny Lee Miller, Lucy Liu. CBS. 2012.

116. <u>Elementary: Lesser Evils</u>. Dir. Colin Bucksey. Perf. Jonny Lee Miller, Lucy Liu. CBS. 2012.

117. <u>Elementary: Flight Risk</u>. Dir. David Platt. Perf. Jonny Lee Miller, Lucy Liu. CBS. 2012.

118. <u>Elementary: One Way to Get Off</u>. Dir. Seith Mann. Perf. Jonny Lee Miller, Lucy Liu. CBS. 2012.

119. Elementary: The Long Fuse. Dir. Andrew Bernstein. Perf. Jonny Lee Miller, Lucy Liu. CBS. 2012.

120. Elementary: You Do It to Yourself. Dir. Phil Abraham. Perf. Jonny Lee Miller, Lucy Liu. CBS. 2012.

121. Elementary: The Leviathan. Dir. Peter Werner. Perf. Jonny Lee Miller, Lucy Liu. CBS. 2012.

122. Elementary: Dirty Laundry. Dir. John David Coles. Perf. Jonny Lee Miller, Lucy Liu. CBS. 2013.

123. Elementary: M. Dir. John Polson. Perf. Jonny Lee Miller, Lucy Liu. CBS. 2013.

124. Elementary: The Red Team. Dir. Christine Moore. Perf. Jonny Lee Miller, Lucy Liu. CBS. 2013.

125. Elementary: The Deductionist. Dir. John Polson. Perf. Jonny Lee Miller, Lucy Liu. CBS. 2013.

126. Elementary: A Giant Gun, Filled with Drugs. Dir. Guy Ferland. Perf. Jonny Lee Miller, Lucy Liu. CBS. 2013.

127. Elementary: Details. Dir. Sanaa Hamri. Perf. Jonny Lee Miller, Lucy Liu. CBS. 2013.

128. Elementary: Possibility Two. Dir. Seith Mann. Perf. Jonny Lee Miller, Lucy Liu. CBS. 2013.

129. Elementary: Déjà Vu All Over Again. Dir. Jerry Levine. Perf. Jonny Lee Miller, Lucy Liu. CBS. 2013.

130. Elementary: Snow Angels. Dir. Andrew Bernstein. Perf. Jonny Lee Miller, Lucy Liu. CBS. 2013.

131. Elementary: Dead Man's Switch. Dir. Larry Teng. Perf. Jonny Lee Miller, Lucy Liu. CBS. 2013.

132. Elementary: A Landmark Story. Dir. Peter Werner. Perf. Jonny Lee Miller, Lucy Liu. CBS. 2013.

133. Elementary: Risk Management. Dir. Adam Davidson. Perf. Jonny Lee Miller, Lucy Liu. CBS. 2013.

134. Elementary: The Woman. Dir. Seith Mann. Perf. Jonny Lee Miller, Lucy Liu. CBS. 2013.

135. Elementary: Heroine. Dir. John Polson. Perf. Jonny Lee Miller, Lucy Liu. CBS. 2013.

136. <u>House M.D.: Small Sacrifices</u>. Dir. Greg Yaitanes. Perf. Hugh Laurie. FOX, 2010.

137. <u>Man of Steel</u>. Dir. Jack Snyder. Perf. Henry Cavill, Amy Adams. Warner Brothers Pictures, 2013.

138. <u>No Place Like Holmes: Series Three: Red Rising</u>. Dir. and Perf. Ross K. Foad. <<u>http://www.nplh.co.uk/episodes.html</u>> 2013.

139. <u>Sherlock: A Scandal in Belgravia</u> ("**ASIB**"). Dir. Paul McGuigan. Perf. Benedict Cumberbatch, Martin Freeman. BBC. 2011.

140. <u>Sherlock: A Study in Pink</u> ("**ASIP**"). Dir. Paul McGuigan. Perf. Benedict Cumberbatch, Martin Freeman. BBC. 2010.

141. <u>Sherlock: The Blind Banker</u> ("**TBB**"). Dir. Euros Lyn. Perf. Benedict Cumberbatch, Martin Freeman. BBC. 2010.

142. <u>Sherlock: The Great Game</u> ("**TGG**"). Dir. Paul McGuigan. Perf. Benedict Cumberbatch, Martin Freeman. BBC. 2010.

143. Sherlock: The Hounds of Baskerville ("**THB**"). Dir. Paul McGuigan. Perf. Benedict Cumberbatch, Martin Freeman. BBC. 2011.

144. Sherlock: The Reichenbach Fall ("**TRF**"). Dir. Toby Haynes. Perf. Benedict Cumberbatch, Martin Freeman. BBC. 2011.

145. Sherlock Holmes. ("**Sherlock Holmes 2010**") Dir. Rachel Lee Goldenberg. Perf. Gareth David-Loyd, Ben Syder. The Asylum, Revolver Entertainment, 2010.

146. Sherlock Holmes. Dir. Guy Ritchie. Perf. Robert Downey Jr., Jude Law. Warner Brothers Pictures, 2009.

147. Sherlock Holmes: A Game of Shadows. ("**Sherlock Holmes: Game**") Dir. Guy Ritchie. Perf. Robert Downey Jr., Jude Law. Warner Brothers Pictures, 2011.

148. Sherlock Holmes faces Death. ("**SH-Death**") Dir. Roy William Neill. Perf. Basil Rathbone, Nigel Bruce. Universal Studios, 1943.

149. Sherlock Holmes in Washington. ("**SH-Washington**") Dir. Roy William Neill. Perf. Basil Rathbone, Nigel Bruce. Universal Studios, 1943.

150. Sherlock Holmes in the 22nd Century: The Fall and Rise of Sherlock Holmes. Dir. Paul Quinn. Perf. Jason Gray-Stanford. Fox Kids, 1999.

151. Sherlock Undercover Dog. Dir. Richard Harding Gardner. Perf. Huey. MDP Worldwide and Westend, 1994.

152. Skyfall. Dir. Mendes, Sam. Perf. Daniel Craig. MGM, Columbia Pictures, 2012.

153. Star Trek. Dir. J.J. Abrams. Perf. Chris Pine, Zachary Quinto. Paramount Pictures, 2009.

154. Star Trek: Into Darkness. ("**Star Trek: ID**") Dir. J.J. Abrams. Perf. Chris Pine, Zachary Quinto, Benedict Cumberbatch. Paramount Pictures, 2013.

155. The Private Life of Sherlock Holmes. Dir. Billy Wilder. Perf. Robert Stephens, Colin Blakely. United Artists, 1970.

156. The Return of Sherlock Holmes. Dir. Kevin Connor. Perf. Margaret Colin, Michael Pennington. CBS, 1997.

157. The Seven-Per-Cent Solution. Dir. Herbert Ross. Perf. Nicol Williamson, Robert Duvall. Universal Studios, 1976.

158. Tom and Jerry Meet Sherlock Holmes. Dir. Spike Brandt and Jeff Siergey. Perf. Malcolm McDowell, Michael York. Warner Brothers Home Video, 2010.

159. Without a Clue. Dir. Thom Eberhardt. Perf. Michael Caine, Ben Kingsley. Orion Pictures/MGM, 1988.

160. Young Sherlock Holmes. Dir. Barry Levinson. Perf. Nicholas Rowe. Paramount Pictures, 1985.

Acknowledgements

First round of thanks must necessarily go to my lovely family – not only for putting up with my Holmes mania for years and years, but also for all the support and encouragement. I know I never say it enough – but I really do owe you all *everything*. Thank you does not seem adequate.

Next, my gratitude turns to the wonderful Tom Ue (I call him "The Scholar") – without whom, this originally-written-as-a-paper-later-turned-into-a-book would have never seen the light of day. Thank you, Tom, *merci beaucoup*. If I were Moriarty, I would say I.O.U. and then give you Aladdin's lamp as *quid pro quo*.

Then I must thank the amazing Calvert Markham (who I still remain greatly in awe of) – not only for the really *cool* foreword, but also for introducing me to Sherlock's London. Thank you, Calvert (and Carole) – you gave me new heroes to worship.

I have to thank the admirable Sumal Surendranath for the Sherlock Holmes Society of India. I have derived much of my inspiration and information from the invigorating discussions of our society. Thank you, Sumalji, for creating SHSI – and for holding it aloft all these years.

I also need to thank the fantastic Bob Gibson for the absolutely amazing cover design – the number of hours I have spent mooning over it is not even remotely funny. Bob, you are every bit of the genius Steve promised you were.

Ultimately, I must thank the gracious Steve Emecz for agreeing to publish this book and for putting up with my idiosyncratic revisions time and again! Steve, you are a rockstar. Actually, you are better than a rockstar.

About the Author

Jayantika Ganguly (a.k.a. Jay) is a corporate lawyer by profession, currently based out of Kolkata, India. She has been Sherlock-crazy since she was twelve. She acts as the General Secretary and Editor for the Sherlock Holmes Society of India. She is also a member of the Sherlock Holmes Society of London and the Czech Sherlock Holmes Society (*Česká společnost Sherlocka Holmese*).

She can be reached at ruling_jay@yahoo.com. For matters related to the Sherlock Holmes Society of India, she is reachable at shsieditors@gmail.com.

Also from MX Publishing

MX Publishing is the world's largest specialist Sherlock Holmes publisher, with over a hundred titles and fifty authors creating the latest in Sherlock Holmes fiction and non-fiction. From traditional short stories and novels to travel guides and quiz books, MX Publishing cater for all Holmes fans. The collection includes leading titles such as *Benedict Cumberbatch In Transition* and *The Norwood Author* the winner of the 2011 Howlett Award (Sherlock Holmes Book of the Year). MX Publishing also has one of the largest communities of Holmes fans on Facebook with regular contributions from dozens of authors.

www.mxpublishing.com

Also from MX Publishing

Our bestselling short story collections 'Lost Stories of Sherlock Holmes' , 'The Outstanding Mysteries of Sherlock Holmes', 'Untold Adventures of Sherlock Holmes' (and the sequel 'Studies in Legacy) and 'Sherlock Holmes in Pursuit'.

www.mxpublishing.com

Links

MX Publishing are proud to support the Save Undershaw campaign – the campaign to save and restore Sir Arthur Conan Doyle's former home. Undershaw is where he brought Sherlock Holmes back to life, and should be preserved for future generations of Holmes fans.

Save Undershaw   www.saveundershaw.com

Sherlockology   www.sherlockology.com

MX Publishing   www.mxpublishing.com

You can read more about Sir Arthur Conan Doyle and Undershaw in Alistair Duncan's book (share of royalties to the Undershaw Preservation Trust) – *An Entirely New Country* and in the amazing compilation Sherlock's Home – The Empty House (all royalties to the Trust).